Published by Ladybird Books Ltd
27 Wrights Lane London W8 5TZ
A Penguin Company
3 5 7 9 10 8 6 4 2
© Jean and Gareth Adamson MCMXCVII

Printed in Italy

Topsy + Tim

Little Lost Rabbit

Jean and Gareth Adamson

Ladybird

When Topsy and Tim looked out of
the window on Wednesday morning,
they saw a black and white rabbit
nibbling their marigolds.

Topsy and Tim heard the doorbell
ring. They ran downstairs and
opened the front door.

Mr Fen who lived next door
was there, holding the rabbit.
"Look what I've found," he said.

The rabbit looked at Topsy and Tim and wiggled his nose.

"Please, may I hold it?" asked Topsy. The rabbit sat quietly with its front paws on Topsy's arm.

"It's very tame," said Mummy. "I wonder who it belongs to?"

"We'll have to ask the neighbours," said Mr Fen.

Dad found a big box for the rabbit to sit in.

"Would it like some of my cornflakes?" asked Tim.

When it was time to go to
playgroup, Topsy and Tim wanted
to stay and play with the rabbit.

"Come on, now," said Mummy. "You can tell Miss Maypole all about the rabbit. One of the children at playgroup might know who it belongs to."

"Does anyone know who might
have lost a black and white rabbit?"
Miss Maypole asked the children.
"Topsy and Tim found one in their
garden this morning."

"It could be Mr Fishwick," said
Lynne. "He lives next door to us.
He keeps black and white rabbits."

When Mummy came to take Topsy and Tim home, Miss Maypole told her about Mr Fishwick.

"We'll see if the rabbit belongs to him this afternoon," said Mummy.

Topsy looked as if she would cry. Tim dragged his toes along the pavement all the way home.

When they got home, the rabbit met
them at the door. It had climbed
out of its box.

All through lunch, the rabbit played round the table legs. It sat up on its back paws so Topsy and Tim could tickle its ears.

After lunch, Mummy put the rabbit inside her zip-bag with a lettuce leaf to nibble. She closed the zip, all but a few centimetres.

The rabbit poked its wiggling nose out of the gap.

"I don't want the rabbit to go," said Topsy.

"I don't, either," said Tim. They were both trying hard not to cry.

"If the rabbit does belong to Mr Fishwick, perhaps he'll let you visit it," said Mummy.

Mr Fishwick didn't live far away. Mummy took the rabbit out of the zip-bag. "Yes," he said, "that's my rabbit. He got out this morning when I opened the hutch."

Topsy and Tim began to cry.

Mr Fishwick looked thoughtful.
"I think my rabbit hutch is getting
too crowded," he said. "Do you
know anyone who could give this
rabbit a good home?"

"We can! We can!" said Topsy and
Tim together.

When they got home again, Mummy said, "Now that he is your rabbit, you must both look after him. You must see that he has water to drink and the right things to eat."

"I'll get him some food now," said Tim.

"And I'll get him some water," said Topsy.

"Is that rabbit still here?" said Dad,
when he came home from work.
Topsy and Tim told him the good news.

"We must give him a name," said Dad.

"We've given him one," said Topsy.

"It's Wiggles," said Tim, "because
his nose wiggles."

"Well then," said Dad, "we must give Wiggles a house."

He took Topsy and Tim to the shed, and they found some wood and wire netting to make a rabbit hutch.

Wiggles sat in his new hutch and
wiggled his nose.

Point to the rabbit pairs.

Help Wiggles to find the way to his
new home.

Tell the story.

Which animals are big?
Which are little?

Match each animal below to
something that rhymes with its name.